TICK TWENTY:

"A COLLECTION OF QUOTES, POEMS, IDEAS, IMAGINATION AND SHORT STORIES"

--RAJDEEP SAHA

ACKNOWLEDGEMENT

A very special thanks to Ishika Ghosh, a beautiful writer with a mastery in her vocabulary who inspired me to write my thoughts and share it with the world. This book is just an illustration of a new perspective to our surroundings.

When I started compiling my quotes and ideas for this book, I realised the excellent journey that I crossed since 2 years. Yes, I got a feeling of excitement and joy as I was seeing all the creative thoughts that grow inside me. Once again I became aware of this faculty that all of us have- and that is to express, to learn and to grow more and more.

And lastly, thanks to myself who took this initiative to write this book and finally publish it. Hope all the readers are going to love this short smiling time a they go through this book.

ABOUT THE BOOK

This book is a collection of short stories, poems, quotes, thoughts and ideas. It's an imagination that connects you to the reality. It' an expression to look at various aspects of our life from love, dream, adventure to solitude, peace and wait. In some portions it describes the beautiful smile a kid brings to you, at other parts it tells you the crude truth about how the society forces someone to become lunatic.

This book is best read in your leisure time and takes just a few minutes to complete it. But once you go through the ticking twenty minutes of imagination, you will surely want to come back to it frequently and take a glimpse of it. This book is not just meant for a carefree reading, but also for a serious introspection. It makes you go inside and look at your inner aspects of how you think and operate about day to day events.

It also brings light to the non-living objects like telephone and tea, how they cover so much parts of our lives and what emotions they trigger inside us. It also romanticises the loss of a lover, and the patience one needs to withstand to again get reunited. A poem named "Death and Birth" makes you look at the spiritual perspective of life. Once you read it you're bound to go through critical thinking about the true nature and purpose of life.

1. //Master-Chef//

Me: Mom, the food is tasteless. There's something less. Please taste it once and check what's wrong.

Mom: Oh! I forgot to put salt in it. Don't worry I will take a pinch and pour into it as much required.

Also me: Mom, ewww, yakk it's too salty! Why did you put so much salt into it? I can't eat it now. Give me water.

Mom: Um, don't worry. I will add some sugar in it. Then you'll be able to eat I guess.

---Raj

Caption: We all are very used to our moms magic. With all the mouth watering food she just feeds our soul with deliciousness. Be it a boy or girl, she knows everyone's way to the heart starts from their stomach. □

It would have been great if we have our mum in every part of our life to fix things. But growing up, we realise that "Oh crap! I need to deal with all these by myself."

TICK TWENTY

Sometimes we feel "What a mess have I created?" And at other times
"Oh! I have everything, but still it's like something missing, something
needs to be added. What is it?"

Well, yeah Forest Gump says it right "Life is like a box of chocolates.
You never know what you gonna get."

But why not try experimenting it in our own way. Let's allow ourselves
to make mistakes, to jumble up everything, to find the missing pieces of
the puzzle, to become detectives to solve the ultimate mysteries.

Let's allow ourselves to be a bit carefree. Not to worry much. And let
things as it is. Let's allow ourselves to dwell in thoughts of past and
future and eventually fall for the beauty of the present.

Be imperfect.
Be vulnerable.
Be insane.

email: rajdeep.master10@gmail.com

2. //**Tune in with Nature**//

Open your ears to the vibrations,
Allow the ship to sink in,
Tired of measuring the infinite depth,
With a needle sized intelligence,
Only to feel lost and start repeating it all again.

Hold your feet firmly on the land,
Or the receding waves will bounce and toss you up,
And Grab you inside the darkness of the past,
Where you'll keep searching for breath,
And the lungs inside will slowly blast.

Allow the approaching waves,
To push you away,
To wash your feet and throw you out.
For they want to save you,
Just trust them and take a moment out.

Stop starring with idle sight,
And sync in with the curly flow,
To sail in the ocean of life,
And get prepared for the upcoming fight.

---Raj

TICK TWENTY

email: rajdeep.master10@gmail.com

3. //**Materialists**//

Sparkling, shinning and glamorous,
Its nature captivates your sight.
Mind dwells at the attractions,
And pulls your attention towards bright,
Vague assumptions masks people,
Thoughts beat up with obsessions; declares:
"Owning materials will give happiness."
But they remain unfulfilled and hollow,
Stays dissatisfied and lost in this turmoil,
Till they give up all lusts and desires,
Because sentient beings expected sense,
From non-sentient, lifeless dull matter.

--Raj

Caption: Seeking for materialistic things, collecting unnecessary objects, filling up with more than required will make you messy and your heart will long for them more and more. You can never get satisfied by chasing material objects.

Rather live for a purpose, live for love, dedicate your life in service that will provide you real contentment. Live as per your nature, the nature of the soul.

email: rajdeep.master10@gmail.com

4. //**Pet and Puppet**//

Pet and Puppet,
Are almost similar.
One is adorable innocent creature,
While the other is
Just a collection of facial feature.

A Pet becomes your family member.
You feed it, love it, beat it,
And kick them out of your window.
But still they would crawl up
To your feet coz they're scared,
Of losing all benefits if they go.

While a puppet enacts any role,
Rolls, flips and dances as per your will.
But even though it stays silent.
Yet can show a whole lot of drama.

Both of them entertains us.
And stay faithful to their master forever.
But never wish to blow life,
Inside your puppet
Because they might not turn out
As trustworthy as your pet.

--Raj

Caption: Pets are also innocent living creatures bounded by laws of nature. Don't treat them as your puppets. Love them, take care of them and they'll show you how to serve you back.

email: rajdeep.master10@gmail.com

5. //**Last Option**//

I'm out of trend,
Unless all others are consumed,
I keep on peeping from the end.
Two ways to treat me:
One- the most fav dish
To be tasted at last.
Or- the worst tasted dish
To be thrown in the trash.

Sometimes I am at the highest value,
To be saved for emergency.
Comes with free choice to accept me,
Or forget my essence completely.
I'm the final chance to put your best,
Reap the perfect remedy,
By giving in me all your faith.

But be careful of me.
Coz while you let go
Of all other options,
For someone important.
However that important one is
Letting go of your importance,
For the other options.

--Raj

email: rajdeep.master10@gmail.com

6. //**Walk Alone**//

Gathering the courage to walk alone,
Demands an ocean of commitment
To pull yourself up everytime
You are broken. But if you survive
You'll become unbreakable and unshakable

Dare to tell your Truth?
They will throw stones at you
Blame you. Call you a misfit.
Others wouldn't even care
And more disempowering is
Who won't take a stand
Even after knowing you are right.

Still for the sake of justice
you've to continue to walk alone
Because others are fearful to support
That they might get attacked
People only stand beside them
Whom they consider to be their own.

--Raj

Caption: As now you know that no-one is your own, so better know
this also that you don't need anyone to believe in you. You've to believe
in yourself. Because you have to walk the path All Alone.

email: rajdeep.master10@gmail.com

7. //**Loneliness**//

Oh red pills, make me drowsy ,
Bring gravity in eyelids.
Remove the blues from the blood,
And inert my awareness deeply.

I'm sick of being ignored,
The longings I have for them, they don't,
Just one hand separation,
And they act as if I was never known.

So many social medias and apps,
Innumerable numbers in contact list,
Yet no-one is in reach; Even-
friends, family all proved to be un-own.

In the world of billions,
No hands to comfort me,
My heart aches; still don't want
To put them handcuffs to be with me.

I am unwanted, they don't like me.
The noises inside are exploding,
 I wish too To be heard by someone
Who doesn't judge me for breathing.

--Raj

email: rajdeep.master10@gmail.com

8. //**Addiction**//

I'll blur your vision,
With the thick smog.
Burn down your skin,
With an electric shock.
Thunderous impulses
In the sky of desires.
From tip to toe it's me
That will conquer you,
Your breath, and eventually
Not let you inhale.
Arrests your judgement capacity,
Becomes your lifelong companion,
And destroy you but never leave.
You'll search for me, crave for me,
Make efforts to get to me.
I'll treasure your brain
with chemicals in the valley.
And slowly eat you up
From within; but you won't know
Because you will only feel pleasure
From me.

--Raj

TICK TWENTY

Caption: There are two types of addictions: Dysfunctional addictions and Healthy addictions

Dysfunctional addictions include smoking, alcohol consumption, drugs etc

Healthy addictions include writing, painting, poetry, creativity which truly helps you transcend your limitations and reach a world where you are your own destiny maker, you can paint it with your own colours and add and subtract as per your will.

Choose wisely which addictions to welcome in your life.

email: rajdeep.master10@gmail.com

9. //**Insane**//

The man was called insane.
Who dared to envision ,
The mental landscapes
That are Alien to others.
Whose wild imagination,
Crossed the boundaries
Of conventional Normalcy.

He would see the patterns,
And challenge for change.
Turned out to be a risk,
For bounded norms in range.
Society humiliated him,
Dismissed the genius within.

He lost hope,
Locked himself up in room.
Took a withdrawal from,
The rude reality
That crushed his soul.
And triggered repeatedly,
To become the psychotic.

Irresistible impulses of highs and lows,
Examined with various names
Of schizophrenia, dementia, depression.
The sane was carried to Asylum;
By the insane's who couldn't hear
The melody running in his head.

--Raj

TICK TWENTY

Caption: Life is tasteless without a bit of Insanity. Dare to be called crazy, get humiliated and dismissed by those who don't have the courage to bend the reality. Be Insane.

email: rajdeep.master10@gmail.com

TICK TWENTY

TICK TWENTY

10. //**An evening walk**//

One evening, me and my father went for a walk. The clouds had painted themselves in crimson, and the lake beside was blowing chilled breeze. While the squirrels fought for nuts, the photographer was trying hard for a click. The white beard people sat on carpet, engrossed with their kings and Aces.

We walked a few steps, crushing the leaves beneath our feet.
At a distance few kids were busy playing lock and keys, hide and seek while the very little ones enjoyed sitting in the lap of their parents.

A child was riding a bicycle passing beside us. My father stopped him and asked, "Hey boy! Will you give me a ride in your cycle?"

He grinned at my father and said, "Once I learn properly, I will surely let u sit at the back. Till then you try to lose some weight.☐"
Me and my father kept on smiling at each other.

--Raj

email: rajdeep.master10@gmail.com

11. //**A Dream**//

The kid desired to reach space,
Looks at the deep blue blanket
Where lies all the celestial sparks,
And within a blink of his eye,
He has stepped on moon,
Flying on asteroids,
Fighting with aliens,
Rescuing the princess,
Of a far unknown galaxy.

That kid grows up,
And realises that he never
Actually reached the moon.
Not even moved any closer.
But he still didn't give up,
Because his only dream,
To go beyond everything
That is pulling his legs down.

--Raj

email: rajdeep.master10@gmail.com

TICK TWENTY

12. //**Death and Birth**//

Death and Birth,
Occurs on Same Bed.
You can't distinguish the two:
For Death is the ultimate Fate,
And Birth is the Beginning
Starring at you
From the End-Gate.

The Bulb can be broken,
Filament can be destroyed
And Lose it's functioning forever.
Yet the electricity never ceases
To exist throughout
the eternal chamber,
Why fear death of flesh?
If life force is what matters.
But if you are attached with the form,
Your all senses will soon get scattered.

Recall during delivery,
Hammer hitting pain inside of her !!
Her screams can criss cross heaven and hell.
But she never refuses to have this suffering.
She wants to hear the tiny lungs breathing,
Because For her
the Life inside is more precious.

--Raj

TICK TWENTY

Caption: Beginnings and endings maynot always be comfortable. But it always brings a new life which is trying to emerge through you, from deep inside you. Let it come out and see the world.
Better to say, make a world of it's own.

email: rajdeep.master10@gmail.com

TICK TWENTY

13. *//A Romantic Mood//*

Wrap the blanket
And feel the warmth,
Hug me from within.
A soft touch of lips,
Wishing luck on forehead,
Will bless you
with togetherness forever.
I'll tickle your feet,
To see the smile in closed eyes.
You place your ears
On my chest,
Sense every beat
Articulating your name.
And let's make a temporary escape,
From all distractions and chaos,
And mix your awareness
With the intoxicating breath,
And sweet smell of each other.

--Raj

email: rajdeep.master10@gmail.com

14. //**Tea**//

A sip of yours,
Relaxes my nerves.
Drowsiness dissapears,
And I return back to senses.
Quite strange is your behaviour,
Sometimes you are addiction
and at times the best cure.
The vessel in which
You are filled in,
Is warm to touch.
But the heat in you
Can burn me up.
Yet I delightfully
Bring you closer,
To my lips, my tongue,
Coz
A sip of yours;
Relaxes my nerves.

--Raj

email: rajdeep.master10@gmail.com

15. //**Telephone**//

Tring-Tring, Tring-Tring:
Pick me up.
Knocking at your attention,
Attend the stuff.
Bringing you all sorts of news:
Good news, Bad news,
Shocking news, Surprising news.
From a quick notification,
To hours of conversation,
Mood of heart depends on the network.
It's a way to reach out
To people who are close
Yet far away physically
All you need is just
Dial up the numbers.
But be careful,
Don't confuse the sequence,
Resulting in a Wrong Number.

--Raj

email: rajdeep.master10@gmail.com

16. //**Know Your Worth**//

 Have you ever wondered why grass are called and treated as unwanted plants, weeds? Why do you think that a healthy green growing plant is called a weed?

It's simple. Because the humans want other plants to get cultivated over there. So, the grass is restricting the growth of other plants.
But does this mean the grass doesn't have any value?
No. So many animals like cows, sheeps, goats, horses, deers etc are feeded on grass.

So, actually grass itself never had a problem.
The problem is in the environment in which it's growing.

--Raj

Caption: So, if you are repeatedly feeling you don't have any value and doubting your worth, then simply understand you are in a wrong environment.
 You are always beautiful, healthy and complete.

email: rajdeep.master10@gmail.com

17. //A Blocked Chat//

I can now tell you all my stories, right from the scratch. And now you won't judge me. I can now tell you how you loved me, hurt me and again and again played with my trust.

I will narrate each small incident that we spent together. I will write about those sleepless nights when you told me about your dreams.

And now you won't get angry on me. You won't use abusive words. I can now share every bit of my emotions, I will laugh, cry, get angry on you and throw all the sword ☐☐ emojis at you, I will kill you, take my revenge and wash my face with your blood. And yeah you won't be aware of any of it now.

I will tell you how my life has been, what I am doing, where I am, whom I met. I will ask about you. Knowing that no one would ever reply from the other end.

--Raj

email: rajdeep.master10@gmail.com

18. //**Solitude**//

I speak to myself,
When I am sad, severe, suffering,
When I am happy, joyful nd smiling,
When the voices outside
And inside are fighting,
When the truth is within,
And lies are surfing.

I speak to myself.
In the midst of thousands,
Or all alone in a room of silence,
Because it's time.
It's time to make the correct choice,
That will direct me to my destination,
And help me shatter the reality,
To rediscover my inner expression.

--Raj

email: rajdeep.master10@gmail.com

19. //**Betrayal**//

I believed in you.
But you have shed my tears,
With the sword stung with deception.
We took blood oath,
To stay together forever,
But you have brought back all fears,
With your act of complete dissimulation.

I believed in you.
To the extent I haven't believed myself,
For you were the one to accept me,
To the extent I couldn't accept myself.
But you now closed the door,
Inside of which lies a voice,
Stabbed with the promises unswore,
And a rage indomitable for sure.

--Raj

email: rajdeep.master10@gmail.com

20. //**First Time**//

First time ever,
There's peace in a Wait,
A stillness in a Fret,
There's courage to Exit,
And liberate from Death.

For the first time ever,
The heart moved so close,
To let me see,
And confess the Truth,
That Your presence is enough
For the Magic to expose.

--Raj

email: rajdeep.master10@gmail.com

TICK TWENTY